JACK'S METTLE

BY: STEPHEN SADLER

*I dedicate this book to my grandson,
Aidan Johnathan Hoenle.*

"Life brings sorrows and joys alike. It is what a man does with them – not what they do to him – that is the true test of his mettle."

— Theodore Roosevelt

Foreword

Well, this is a little embarrassing…

I've been dead since 1952 and no one has ever asked me to say a word until now.

When my great-nephew Stephen reached out to me and suggested I write the foreword to his little book about me, I nearly told him to sod off. I was never much of a writer, and though I could spin a pretty fair yarn some nights at the pub, I never felt qualified to put my story down on paper.

But, now that Stephen has gone to the trouble of telling my story, I think it's only fair to return the favour and offer my perspective on his book - for what it's worth.

There is a part of me that still marvels that anyone would even be interested in a muddy football match played over 100 years ago. I was only a boy when that moment passed, and a bit of a nutter back then to boot - But being a goalkeeper, that was to be expected.

After reading Stephen's book, I began to realize why he asked me to write this foreword. For the day I became a champion in 1912, was the day I became more than just a great uncle – I became a lasting symbol of hope for those who would come after me.

History fades when there is no one left to carry it on, and ghosts go silent when no one remembers them. Fortunately, I have watched our little Stephen all his life, through the good and bad times, the tears and laughter, the wins and losses, and light and the dark. At every step, I was there, making sure that Stephen and his family earned their mettle, while ensuring they would never be left behind.

Fortunately for me, Stephen felt my presence throughout his life and kept my memory alive within these pages.

Now, you are about to embark on a journey that crosses through time, overlapping the lives of two men who never met, but shared a bond that bridged the gap across generations. This is their story of pain, struggle, and the ultimate triumph of the human spirit.

I am grateful that Stephen has seen fit to tell my tale. He is a good lad with a real gift for storytelling.

Of course, I'm a bit biased, but I think you'll enjoy it.

Cheers,

Jack Cooper

Prologue

I *never met* Jack. I had heard the stories a thousand times and even held his medal in my own little hands. In my family, Jack Cooper was a legend, a mythical figure of epic proportions, who quietly led Barnsley to the 1912 FA Cup Championship.

Born John Holloway, he was also the same scrapper who took on Millwall supporters, single-handedly battling the crowd who threw rubbish at him from the stands.

That was Jack — a conundrum — both tough and tenacious while being a thoughtful, caring man who knew the importance of friends and family.

Jack Cooper was a guiding ghost who haunted my life from early in my childhood. A phantom who helped this kid from Nottingham muddle through the muck and mire of having to grow up English in Canada, before emigrating to the United States.

There were tears, anger, and laughter at almost every stage of my upbringing, yet the spectre of Jack Cooper and his championship medals loomed large in the background.

Football (aka soccer), hockey, and other sports became metaphors for the daily battles against aggressive bullies, unaware teachers, and my undiagnosed dyslexia. Those games and that competition lit a fire under my competitive spirit and Jack's ghost was always there, fanning the flames.

However, this is less of a story about my life, but a story of how the legacy and legend of those that have gone before us can make a lasting, positive impact on our lives.

Through Jack's great deeds, and the stories that surround him, I have been blessed with all the love and support I ever needed to carry on.

This story is for everyone who has ever failed, fallen, or felt they didn't have the strength to get up again. This is the story of my family through the generations, illustrating how our lives are all interconnected and intertwined in layers upon layers over time. For, in the end, we all impact each other in so many different ways without ever really knowing.

Ultimately, this is a tale about you, and me, and what we all can learn from Jack Cooper's indomitable spirit.

This is the story of Jack's Mettle.

1

Into the Mist

T he girls were really on their game today. As I stood on the sideline, I couldn't have been prouder, watching the ebb and flow of the game roll back and forth in waves across the pitch.

The Under-13 team that came to me as green, raw recruits the past autumn had gelled into something really special by spring. Now, I was watching a confident, experienced group of young players challenge every opponent, every minute of the game, driving us directly to the top of the division.

It was at the very moment little Willow had her first breakaway that it happened. The thought of my Great Uncle Jack popped into my head as I cheered our young striker speeding down the left side of the pitch toward our opponent's goal.

Suddenly I wasn't just a coach on a Saturday morning sideline in Michigan. Somehow, some way, I was 10 years old, back in my bedroom in Nottingham...

◆

As I rubbed the sleep out of my eyes, I noticed my black and white football up against the far wall of my bedroom.

Then realizing what day it was, I jumped up on the bed and screamed, "EH UP, IT'S SATURDAY... NO SCHOOL, FOOTBALL WITH ME MATES!"

Excited, I leapt off the bed and ran over to my closet to find my footballer's kit. As I ripped through the hanging clothes, I found my red and green Nottingham Forest kit, right next to my cub scout uniform.

Quickly I took off my pyjamas, put on my kit, and headed downstairs. As I looked out the big front window, I could see that it had rained overnight.

"Good, only a little drizzle and light fog," I said to myself smiling. In Nottingham terms, just another perfect day for English football with me mates. You see, in England, if we let the weather dictate what we did, we'd never leave the house. Especially on Saturday, we never cared about the weather, because we just loved football. Every Saturday meant getting up early, and racing to Jesse Boot school grounds to meet with my mates, and get right filthy.

"Tah Mum," I yelled, running out the door with food from breakfast still in my mouth.

"Hold up, where are you goin'? she shouted.

"Jesse Boot Mum. Remember Football with Darrel and Gloss," I yelled back as I got to our front gate.

"Well alright, but remember we're goin' to Grandma and Grandad Whitehead's house tonight!"

"I know, I remember Mum."

"Good, we need to be there by seven, so be home before five for din din," she explained, turning to go back inside.

"Right then, Tah Mum," and I slammed the gate and started running full speed down Eastdale Road past all the red brick houses and gardens that looked like carbon copies of each other.

"Watch out for cars, it's quite foggy, Stephen," she shouted, as she closed the door.

"I will, Mum," I shouted back now running even faster.

As I turned the corner onto Avon Road I could see the pitch through the black-painted wrought iron fence of the Jesse Boot Primary School playgrounds. The closer I got, the clearer I could see two small figures running near the goal at the far right of the pitch.

Nice, Gloss and Darrel are already here, I thought to myself. *Today will be brilliant.*

As a child, I had great friends. Darrel was one of those nutters that loved to play keeper. For his young age of 10, he had a fairly stocky athletic build, with dark hair and dark eyes.

Gloss on the other hand was very lean, blond, with blue eyes and kind of looked like Draco Malfoy if you follow Harry Potter. He was an incredible ball handler and shooter.

Me, I was nothing special, I just loved the game so much that I didn't care what position I played — just not a goalkeeper. I thought of my old Uncle Jack, playing keeper for Barnsley and winning the FA Cup. However, I didn't feel tough enough to think I could ever reach those heights, so playing keeper was out of the question.

As I entered through the old wrought iron gates, the fog appeared to be getting thicker.

I love the fog, I thought to myself, kicking the ball onto the wet pitch. As I looked down, I smiled at my replica Georgie Best football boots, that my sister, Jennifer, had bought me before she had left for Canada. Jennifer was 10 years older than me, so it was like having another Mum, for play purposes only. For some reason, she just loved taking me on shopping sprees, in downtown Nottingham.

"Ay-up," shouted Gloss, as he crushed the ball past Darrel from the penalty spot.

"A ow ya gowin," I replied. "Is anyone else comin'?"

"Nay, just us today mate, must be afraid of the bloody fog," laughed Darrel, diving in the mud for the ball.

"It's you against me mate, and Darrel will play keep," chimed Gloss.

"Alright," I replied, reluctantly.

Gloss was an ace player and one of the best in the school for his age. He was also the school comedian and loved to play pranks which in some cases got him into trouble. One time in school at lunch, we were all sitting together. For some unknown reason, there was no adult to monitor the room so all the students were getting louder and louder, especially Gloss.

Suddenly, one of the male teachers came around the corner and screamed, "SHUT YOUR CAKE HOLES, YOU SOUND LIKE A BUNCH OF FARM ANIMALS." Quickly the room went quiet. After about 10 seconds of silence had passed, the teacher gleamed with satisfaction and walked towards the door to leave the room. I noticed Gloss had that look in his eyes. Suddenly, he smirked and blurted out a loud, "MOOOOOOOO," then followed by another mate. Needless to say, Gloss and my other mate were sent to see the Headmistress and probably got caned. Yes, caning was a common occurrence back then. I once got it for just making a goalpost out of a tree branch. Trust me, I never touch the greenery again, probably why I hate gardening.

As I started to dribble, Gloss trapped my ball and looked down at my feet.

"Sadler you berk, are those really Georgie Best boots?" he teased, then took the ball off me and scored on Darrel

"Best's a bloody tosser you know that," laughed Darrel, and they both chuckled. "Besides you're not a Man U supporter, you love Forest."

Both were now tugging at my red Nottingham Forest jersey.

"You takin' the piss. The jersey is from my sister," I replied.

"You wearing your sister's clothes mate," chuckled Gloss now standing directly in front of me.

"No, I mean she bought it for me," I tried to explain, which was a complete waste of breath.

"Bollocks, you're wearing your sister's jumper," laughed Gloss, now dribbling the ball all around the penalty box.

"Well, why do you berks support the Spurs, you don't even live close to London," I exclaimed while pointing at their shirts and failing to defend myself.

"Simple, because they're bloody brilliant mate. They'll win the cup way before Forest does," replied Gloss, flipping the ball over Darrel's head and kicking it in the back of the net before it hit the ground.

"Anyway who cares, let's PLAY," yelled Darrel. "If the fog gets any thicker we won't be able to see."

"Since when did that stop us, I love the fog," I replied trying to take my ball back from Gloss.

"You're barmy anyways Sadler," replied Gloss, laughing.

We began tackling, diving in the mud, pushing, tripping, and pretty well anything to gain an advantage. As the hours went on the fog continued to get thicker and the winter twilight was making it almost impossible to see, but no one wanted to stop playing.

Then I heard a voice shout through the fog, "Stephen, Stephen, are you there?"

Recognizing the voice I shouted back, "Dad is that you?" I watched as his silhouette entered through the wrought iron gate and out from the mist.

"Bloody hell Stephen, your Mum's a nervous wreck, you should have been home hours ago," he shouted, now walking onto the pitch towards us.

"Why, what time is it?" I asked.

"It's past din-din time. Don't you remember we're going to your Grandma Whitehead's house tonight?" he replied.

"Oh yeah, but can we give Gloss and Darrel a ride home, it's on the way," even though that wasn't quite true.

"Alright, but hurry up then."

"We're coming," I replied, and we grabbed our gear and ran towards my Dad's Triumph Herald station wagon that he also used for his struggling interior decorating business. My Dad was the best. He was not a big man, but he had a huge heart. The kind of man that would do anything for anyone and ask for nothing in return.

"You're all soaking wet. Aren't you knackered?" asked Dad, putting his hand on my hair and then feeling the back of my drenched Nottingham Forest jersey.

"No Dad we're not tired, we love playing," I beamed and we

all climbed into the car.

"There's no doubt about that lad," he smiled. "You remind me of your mum's Uncle Jack — never could get him off the pitch either.

Those were the last words I heard before being pulled back into the present.

♦

... A roar rose up from the sideline, waking me from my stupor. My assistant coach and daughter, Noelle, jumped up as Willow rocketed the ball just outside the right goalpost. The final whistle blew, followed by a low groan from our parents.

Nil-1 Loss.

2

Life Lesson

I ***wasn't sure*** what called me back to those memories of Nottingham. But something triggered it, and I wanted to find out why. The evening found me sitting on the edge of my bed, opening up the creaky jewellery case. It was still covered in the same dust as when it was given to me.

Inside, I found the thing that had fascinated me since childhood — Jack's medal. It has been so long since I had held the precious object in my hand. It felt cool and familiar, like a golden memory resurrected from days gone by.

It wasn't a very large piece, small enough to fit in my palm, not even 2 inches in diameter.

The medallion was embossed on the front with the figures of two footballers standing on either side of the crest of the Football Association Challenge Cup, complete with the Royal Coat of Arms of the United Kingdom. A banner ran underneath the boots of the players, across the face of the medallion, which read, "1912."

On the back side, intricate filigree work was etched around

its edges with lines inscribed in the centre:

English Cup
Winners
Barnsley FC
J. Cooper
FOOTBALL

As I ran my index finger along its raised edges, I couldn't help but think about what it took to win England's highest prize in its most beloved sport.

And Jack was right there, in the heat of the battle, the centre of it all ... head up, arms raised, eyes focused ... goaltending.

◆

I always loved going over to my grandparent's house, especially in the fall when horse chestnut trees on Wells Road were dropping the next potential king conker — buckeyes in America.

The largest and strongest conker was the key to controlling the playground at school. My Granddad would help me drill a hole in the conker and put a string through it with a large knot.

The game was simple — one person would dangle the

conker on the string, while the other would swing their stringed conker using a downward stroke to hit the other one and knock it off the string. It might sound easy but trying to hit your mate's conker was a lot harder than it might sound. Over the years, I had found several king conkers from trees near my Grandma's front yard.

They lived in a council house and their backyard was small but usually manicured and in the summer was lined with flowers, especially roses. At the very back was an old bomb shelter, from the war, where Granddad kept his gardening tools and other lawn equipment.

Our visit on this particular day was different than all the rest, as my parents had decided to leave England and follow my sisters, who had moved to Canada. Little did I know that this would be the last time I would ever see my grandparents again.

I can't blame my parents for wanting to move to Canada. The economy was horrible, my Dad's business was struggling, and both of their daughters had emigrated to another country to start a new life. There was also a looming nuclear threat from the Cold War, and because my Dad served in the Royal Air Force during World War II, he didn't want Mum and I to experience any more conflicts.

This was one of the few times, I just sat quietly in their living room listening to my parents explain the move, to my Grandma Whitehead. As usual, the house smelled like old furniture. The living room was decorated with colourful flowered wallpapered decor that was a blend from the 1940s, '50s, and '60s. Black and white family photos hung on the side wall, including military photos of Granddad during war times.

"Well Connie it all sounds well, but where did you and Alf decide to live in Canada?" my Grandma asked.

"Etobicoke, it's a part of Toronto," answered Mum.

"It's expensive in Toronto isn't it, how you goin' to afford that?" she asked.

"It's cheaper than here Mum, besides at first we'll be staying with Jennifer and Colin," explained Mum.

"What about work?" she asked.

"Colin is helping Alf to get a job in Toronto, everything will be alright," replied Mum, but I could sense the uncertainty in her voice.

"What about Stephen?" Grandma asked looking over at me. "How will he get on?"

"Oh, he's young, he'll adapt, he actually wants to go, he really misses Jennifer," replied Dad.

"Right Stephen, do you want to go?" asked Grandma.

"Ah, yes, I think so," I replied, but in reality, I didn't understand the magnitude of what I was saying. I really missed Jennifer, but I didn't realize how much I was going to miss everything else we were about to leave behind.

All I knew about the west was from American television and

I was hooked on *Lost in Space, Scooby Doo, Land of the Giants, The Banana Split Show*, and *Abbott and Costello*. It's very interesting and a little scary how the media can affect our decisions at such a young age.

"Stephen, come here ... HURRY UP," shouted my Granddad, from his spot in the kitchen. That old table and chair up against the sterile white plaster wall.

I jumped up and ran from the living room into the kitchen. Once there, he turned from the table to face me. Granddad Whitehead was not a tall man, at about 5 feet 5 inches, but he was known in Nottingham as being someone not to be messed with. He was a highly decorated soldier in World War I where he served in the tank division, and in World War II reenlisted in the Navy at 45 years of age and became a physical education instructor. After the war, he opened and ran his own tin smith business for many years. His forearms looked like Popeye's with Navy tattoos on both arms. I even remember watching him do a backflip off the steps at the age of 70.

"Why you so filthy?" he asked, glaring at my Nottingham Forest shirt and the dirt still on my socks and knees. "Come here," and he pulled me closer to him.

"I was playing football with me mates, Granddad," I smiled.

"You're just like your old Uncle Jack ... Maybe someday you'll come to your bloody senses, and be a County supporter."

"Granddad, I like Forest because of the colours, Jennifer

bought me the kit," I replied.

"Your sister is a field hockey player, what does she know about football," he sneered. "Besides colours, Blah — black and white are all you need, my lad."

Not knowing how to respond, I just stood there in silence. Then he grabbed my arm again and asked, "Ahrode ay-yo now?"

"I'm almost 10," I answered.

"Ten, ay. Do ya know how to fight?" he asked staring at me with his dark piercing eyes.

"Not really," I replied, trying not to make full eye contact.

"Then put up ya dukes!"

"Whut?" somewhat confused and a little intimidated.

"Go ahead lad, don't be frittin," he pushed.

"I'm not frightened," I gulped, holding my hands just below my face.

"Then git 'em up higher," he growled.

But before I even finished raising my hands, "SMACK," right in my nose. I screamed as blood started coming out, prompting my Mum to run into the kitchen to see what in the world was going on.

By then tears were pouring out of my eyes and I could barely see.

"WHUT THE HELL YOU DOIN DAD?!" she yelled at him.

"Whut," and he laughed shrugging his shoulders. "Just havin' a bit of fun with him."

Mum grabbed me by the arm and pulled me from the kitchen and back into the living room. As I sat still on the edge of the settee she cleaned up my blood using a combination of my Mum's and my Grandma's white cotton handkerchiefs. Slowly my eyes started to clear and I noticed that my Dad had gone into the kitchen to have a word with Granddad.

"What's up with ya?" I heard my Dad say.

"Toughening him up Alf," Granddad replied. "Make 'em right rough 'n tumble, like his goaltending uncle."

They continued to talk, but it was hard for me to hear them now that I was back in the living room.

"So, whut happened lad?" Grandma asked, now sitting beside me on the settee.

"Granddad asked me if ... (sniff) ... I knew ... (sniff) ... how to fight," I explained, still upset and in a bit of pain.

"Then whut happened?" she asked.

"He ... (sniff), he told me to put up me dukes,"

Now she grabbed me by the chin and turned my head towards her. She then wiped my nose with a bit of spit on her handkerchief.

"... and whut did you do?"

"I put them up, then he told me to get 'em higher," I mumbled, still sniffling, while she finished wiping away the remaining blood.

"... and," still continuing to prod.

"He punched me and gave me a bloody nose!" I snapped back, as I was starting to feel annoyed with her prodding.

Then she slowly leaned forward, "Ay, then next time, lad, you betta get ya dukes higher," smiled Grandma.

At the time, I thought they had both gone bloody bananas. They had always treated me like gold prior to this and Grandad had never laid a hand on me before.

"Did ya hear me?" she commanded.

"Yes, I'll get 'em up, Grandma," I replied, now calming down as the pain and blood had gone. In reality, he didn't hit me very hard. If he did he would have easily broken my nose.

As crazy as it sounds though, he did it in love. It was the last impression he could make to help prepare me for the hard road he knew would lie ahead. I also believe he knew, that it was the last time he would ever see me.

Grandma reached over to hand me another hanky and I noticed the gold medal glistening around her neck. It was her brother's English Championship football medallion. Since his death, Grandma wore the medallion with great pride and remembrance.

"Can I see Uncle Jack's medal, Grandma?" I asked.

"Sure lad," she replied.

As I reached out, I noticed how well-preserved it was.

"Jackie was a great man, Stephen, MVP in 1912 for Barnsley, you know," she smiled.

I had heard parts of the story many times before, but I was really too young to know who, what, or even where Barnsley was. All I knew was Barnsley was somewhere further north, and that winning an FA cup medal in England was the next best thing to making it to heaven.

"So where is Barnsley?" I asked.

"Oh that's in Yorkshire me duck," she answered.

"He's from Nottingham. Why didn't Jack play for Forest,"

"YERWOTT!" yelled Granddad still in the kitchen, his ears sharp as ever. "You know we don't say that name in this house, and it's time you took off that bloody Forest jersey."

"SHUT YA GOB AND LEAVE HIM ALONE!," Grandma yelled back into the kitchen. "Don't worry about him Luv. You know he's an old Nott's County nutter. He hates your Forest kit lad, why do you bother wearing it here? It just gets him goin'."

"Gerroff woman, I can still hear ya tongue wagging!" Grandad yelled back and then continued talking to my Dad.

"What was Jack like, Grandma?" I asked.

"Well that is a very long story my lad," she replied.

"Tell me ... please," I begged.

"Alright," she said sweetly, as I still held the medal in my hand. "Let's start at the beginning..."

3
The Long Goodbye

G*randma Whitehead was* a natural storyteller. She knew how to spin a yarn with the best of them, especially when the tale she told was close to her heart — like the legend of Jack Cooper.

As I sat beside her, listening intently, the world faded away, and I was transported back to the days of her youth...

His Christian name was John, but I always called him Jackie. He was the youngest of my three brother's along with Arthur and Alec Junior. We were all very close, but back in the 1890s, the times were very different for me, duck.

Like most of the families in Sneinton, at that time, we didn't have much. We were very, very poor. It was the end of the Victorian era and the industrial revolution was upon us.

Me Dad worked all day long in an iron foundry but he received very little pay. When school was done I would work in

Nottingham lace market close to the Castle, while Arthur also worked nights in the iron foundry. Unfortunately, our combined wages were barely enough to support the four of us.

It seems just like yesterday when my Mum and Dad told us all that Jack and Alec would be going to live with another family.

It was about 9 p.m. and Arthur and I had just walked home together from work. Jack and Alec were sitting in their pyjamas watching Dad stoke the coal into the fireplace on the far wall of our small dimly lit living room. Like most nights Mum was reading to them under the candlelight.

"Ay up, you two, I'm glad you're home early.," she said looking up from the book and trying to smile.

"Ay, Mum," I replied.

"Come here, the both of you, I want to have a little chat," she sighed.

"Alright Mum, but let me get a bite first," replied Arthur, opening the nearly bare larder (pantry) in the adjacent kitchen.

"You two, off to bed, we need to speak to your older brother and sister," she said slapping Jackie on the behind as he giggled.

"But Mum, just a little longer, I love this part," insisted Alec.

"I've read this story to you many times me lads, don't you two ever get sick of it?" she asked.

"No, please Mum just finish this chapter," pleaded Jackie.

"Sure son."

That's strange, I thought to myself, Mum usually never gives in to the lads at bedtime. But tonight was different, and without argument, she continued reading the rest of the chapter and even a little of the next.

As I sat in the big chair next to the settee I watched her quietly close the book while Jackie fell to sleep on her lap. At that moment, Arthur walked back into the living room chewing on a piece of bread and butter.

"So what do want to gab about Mum?" he asked in his usual direct manner.

"Shhhh," replied Mum. "He's asleep," and she brushed Jackie's hair with her hand as he still lay motionless on her lap.

"Come on hun, let's get them to bed," whispered Dad, as he bent over to pick up Jackie. Alec was still wide awake and he jumped up and started towards the stairs with my Dad carrying Jackie and Alec following close behind.

"Go on you little bugger," he chuckled as Alec ran up the stairs carrying his light.

"So whut is it all about, Mum?" I asked again. We could still hear both Jackie and Alec giggling with Dad upstairs.

"Deary, you might want to sit down," she quietly replied. and I sat down on the small settee facing my favourite chair to the left of the old brick fireplace.

"Why, whut's wrong Mum?" I asked, now feeling quite nervous.

"Well, I'll get right to it then. We have to put Jackie and Alec up with another family,"

"Whut, I don't understand, whut does that mean Mum, why do they have to leave?" I asked frantically. At that moment, Dad came down the stairs and sat in the other chair to the right of the fireplace.

"We just can't afford to feed everyone lass, especially with the price of coal," explained Dad.

"But we're all working, there must be some other way," Arthur pleaded, realizing the implications of what was about to happen.

"No, I'm sorry, there is no other way. A family has offered to help take care of Jackie and Alec," she responded, trying to console.

"How can you let them go? I implored, now starting to cry.

"It's alright lass, the Denmans are a good family and they will take care of them, it doesn't have to be permanent," she continued to explain.

"But there has to be another way," I begged. As I looked over my Mum's shoulder and into the stairwell, I could see Jackie and Alec sitting on the stairs and listening to the conversation.

"No, Mable, me Luv, there is no other way," she replied, but I could see the pain in her eyes, turning her head away to hide her emotions.

"When are they leaving?" I asked.

"On Saturday," she replied.

"Saturday, two days, why so fast Mum?" cried Arthur.

"Look me luvs, I didn't want you to have long to worry about it. Besides, we will visit them all the time, your Dad and I just want them to have the best chance possible."

Saturday came quickly. I still remember the sad little faces of Jackie and Alec standing on the front steps of the cobblestoned sidewalks while my Mum kneeled in front of them kissing their cheeks.

"You lads be good, right, remember it's not permanent, and we will visit all the time," she reassured.

"I know Mum," replied Jackie, sniffling.

"Listen, lad, I want you to continue playing your game," she instructed, wiping a tear from Jackie's cheek. Football was Jackie's love and for as far back as I could remember he was always kicking something around.

"I will Mum," replied Jackie, as a black horse-drawn carriage slowly pulled up in front of the house.

Slowly the carriage door swung open and a man's voice yelled, "Well, let's not dilly dally lads, come on git in."

"A horse carriage, Mum, they have a bleedin' horse carriage," revered Jackie.

"Yes, and watch ya mouth. That's Mr Denman, you will be living with them now, so go on," and unwillingly she pushed her sons away from her and towards the man who grabbed their arms and lifted them and their small bags into the carriage.

Arthur and I stood quietly beside Mum as I watched her turn her head so Jackie and Alec couldn't see her cry. In disbelief, we continued to wave as the carriage slowly started to move.

"Remember, no matter where you go, or what you do. We will always love you."

... and the carriage gained speed and moved further and further away until Jackie and Alec were gone.

... I looked up at Grandma as she finished her story, noticing the soft tears rolling down below her cat-eye glasses.

"Life is full of changes, Stephen. Some of them are beautiful and exciting, and some of them are horrible and painful. Most of the time, you get a little bit of both. Do you understand, Luv?"

"Yes, Grandma, I do," I quietly replied.

My grandmother smiled, as I watched her roll Jack's medal over and over again between her fingers.

"Just remember what me mum and dad told Jackie and Alec — No matter where you go, or what you do. We will always love you."

"I know, Grandma," I smiled back. "I know."

4

Becoming Jack Cooper

*L*ife for Jack was a roller coaster ride of ups and downs.
As the family tells it, Little Jackie was always a bit of an odd
duck. He was a very active child and had trouble sitting still in
church, school, and even in the parlour when company came
over for a Sunday visit. The Denman's were good people and
Jackie regularly visited with his family at his old home. My
Grandma's family loved him, and so did the Denman's. It was
through that love he made a commitment to take care of the
ones he loved. He was just that kind of person, and no one was
going to be left behind on his watch.

Mum and Dad Denman soon learned that it was always best
to send Jackie outside with the other children, where he could
burn off some of his excess energy.

As Jackie grew, he was able to channel some of that extra
energy into sports. He loved anything that allowed him to run
and compete with the rest of the lads. Cricket was fun, but
lacked the contact Jackie craved. Rugby fit the bill, but the
young boy grew tired of scrum after scrum. "Too barbaric," he

stated. "Football is more refined."

Of all the sports he played, football was his love and passion. There was something about the balance between skill, speed, and creativity that sparked Jackie's imagination. He wasn't the fastest runner, but his reflexes were uncanny. He moved like a jackrabbit and could pivot on a dime.

These natural gifts combined with his fearless, daring personality made him one of the greatest goalkeepers to ever come out of Nottingham.

Opponents hated going up against Jack. At 5 feet 10 inches it wasn't his size that was intimidating, but a steely, determined look that let you know you were in for a world of hurt if you dare cross into his goal area.

Nothing seemed to deter young Jackie from making it into the professional leagues, where he would take his place among the top football stars of the day.

It didn't take him long to make his mark and at the tender young age of 19, Jack "Cooper" began his football career with Sutton Town before joining Second Division Barnsley toward the end of the 1908 season. The young goaltender made his Football League debut against Clapton Orient on Boxing Day, leading the team to his first victory.

We're not really sure, where and when he took on the name Cooper, some say it was a family he stayed with during the amateur leagues, but Cooper became his professional name, thus making the myth even more elusive.

Cooper made seven more appearances in his debut season as an understudy to Tommy Thorpe. But by the end of the year, Jack would take over as first-string goalkeeper, ready to start the new season in September 1909.

The next few years were rough for Jack. His play wasn't outstanding the following season, and a broken leg kept him out of action for the entire 1910-11 campaign. In fact, he wouldn't return for gameplay until November 1911, when his odyssey toward the FA Cup Championship would begin.

There was nothing but death that was going to stop Jack from succeeding at his craft, and the 1911-12 season was an uphill climb all the way. Cooper played brilliantly in almost every game to get Barnsley to the qualifying game against Swindon in 1912. Whoever won the match would host West Bromwich Albion for the cup final.

That day, it was clear Jack was one of the heroes to be lauded for his outstanding play, leading his team to a 1-0 victory. His many saves included stopping a penalty shot from Swindon's Striker Brown and deflecting a sure goal from Jefferson over the top crossbar.

Ultimately, 1912 would prove to be the season that Jack Cooper really came into his own. After a year of injuries and personal setbacks, the gritty kid from Nottingham had fought his way back against all odds to arrive on the threshold of greatness.

Of course, it's one thing to reach the doorway of success, and quite another to walk on through to the other side.

5

Leaving on a Jet Plane

*M*rs *Grant was* my level 5 teacher at Jesse Boot
Primary School. She was around 30 years of age, somewhat
friendly, but definitely maintained control of the classroom.

She was a lot different than my previous teachers, and had
no tolerance for what they called, "my left-handedness."

I was just a kid that loved to draw, but I couldn't read. The
Headmistress's solution for my reading problems was to place
me out into the unheated hallway, where I couldn't be
distracted. The problem was, this just amplified my anxiety and
made it harder to complete my assignments. The real problem
wasn't distractions or lack of focus. It turned out to be several
physical issues that we didn't know about until many years
later. There was no way Mrs Grant would've known that, and
I've never blamed her for it.

In retrospect, she wasn't equipped to handle literacy
disorders. No one was back then. So I needed an out, and
moving to Canada, turned out to be the option.

As the morning class ended, for outdoor playtime (recess),

some of my classmates passed by my temporary hallway desk. I could hear them talking about me as they walked by.

"I hear he's going to Canada," one of the girls whispered to her friends.

"Yes, I heard there are killer grizzly bears there," replied the other.

As I followed my classmates outside, I could tell the word had definitely gotten out that I was moving. Many of my friends were now asking lots of questions, but I really didn't have any answers.

I didn't have the foggiest idea about bears, moose, Niagara Falls, Mounties, or anything related to the Great White North.

The only thing I knew, was that I would see my sister Jennifer again, who I missed so much. Plus, I would escape the grip of Mrs Grant and the dreaded Headmistress.

As I scanned the playground there was no sign of Gloss and Darryl.

That's unusual, I thought to myself, as they were always playing football on the asphalt. I felt empty inside, yet I wasn't sure why.

So that afternoon, on my way home from school, I decided to take a small detour and drop by Gloss's grandmother's house, where he often went after school. Actually, it was more than a little detour, her house was quite far from my house. With it being February, the weather was dreary and cold.

Luckily there wasn't any fog or rain and I loved to walk. Walking made me feel free like I was heading someplace special.

As I walked, I passed rows and rows of semi-detached brown brick homes, all with small little gardens contained by brick walls or large hedges.

I wonder what the houses are like in Canada? I thought to myself.

As I arrived at the front door of his grandmother's home, I could hear someone moving around inside.

Good, they're home, I thought as I reached out to knock on the door.

The knocker created a satisfying sound from the old solid wooden door, and quickly someone started to unlock the latch and open the door. It was Paul's mum.

"Hello, Ma'am," I said.

"Oh, hello, Stephen, Are you here to see Paul?" she asked.

"Ah, Gloss," I replied. "Sorry, yes, I mean Paul."

She smiled, "Hold on, he's here somewhere. I'll get him,"

As I waited, I glanced back toward a couple of kids playing across the road.

Nobody I know, I thought to myself, and I turned back towards the front door, and watched Gloss, slowly approach the front door from the darkness of the hallway.

"Hey Mate."

"Whut you want?" Gloss replied, in an annoyed tone.

"Can you come out and play?" I asked.

"Whut's the sense?" he scowled.

"Sense?"

"You're leavin' for Canada," he huffed.

"Well yeah, I know but that's not for a few weeks," I explained.

"Whatever, you're still going, aren't ya?" he replied.

Then it hit me hard. I wasn't just going on a vacation trip to Skegness. This was another continent, I might never see my friends again. I knew he was upset, but I was just too young to know how to respond to him, so I just stood there silent, like a lump on a log.

Finally, he sighed, "I'll see ya," and he firmly closed the door and I walked away, towards my house, completely numb.

The sad image of his forlorn, 10-year-old face haunted me for years.

After about 20 minutes of walking, I arrived at my home and stopped directly in front of the house. I carefully looked at the only place I'd ever known as home, and the place I would soon be leaving.

"Are we making the right decision?" I said to myself.

Over the next couple of weeks, everything accelerated —

especially packing.

"Stephen!" Dad yelled up the stairs.

"Yes, Dad?" I replied, from my bedroom.

"Did you pick out the toys your bringing to Canada?" he asked.

"No, not yet, but I'm pretty sure I know," I answered.

Mum and Dad had made it clear, I could only take three small toys and the rest had to stay. It was something about the weight. So, I selected my orange Action Man parachute and placed two Action Man figures, with kung fu grip, in the middle of the chute with few accessories, and a bit of Lego.

"What about my Super Striker and other games?" I asked.

"No way, too big," my Dad replied. "But Mr Ocibovs' sons next door would probably love them.

The Ocibov family had just moved in next door and had emigrated from Italy. Their kids literally had nothing. So instead of leaving the toys for the sale, I decided to give them all of my toys. It was hard for a 10-year-old to make these kinds of decisions over such a short period of time.

That said, I remember how happy their faces were when we handed them the boxes of toys that I'd been spoiled with. Little did I know, we would soon become immigrants in another country, facing similar feelings of anxiety and excitement.

D-day finally came. It was March 2, 1975. The sky was pitch black as we loaded our bags into the cab.

"So London?" Asked the cab driver.

"Yes sir, off to Canada," my Dad responded with a smile.

I had already been warned that the car ride was about three hours long, and the plane ride was another eight hours, which didn't include boarding time and immigration processing when we landed in Canada. The trip length would feel like a lifetime to a kid, but I was so excited to see Jennifer, I really didn't care.

Upon arrival in London, we stayed the night at a hotel before flying out the next day. The last meal we had in England was scallops, which was a luxury item back then, but Dad wanted me to enjoy the trip, as much as possible.

He even bought me my first ballpoint pen and pencil set, so I could draw on the plane. Everyone called my dad Alf, and he was a very thoughtful and loving father.

My Mum, Connie, was wonderful too, but World War II had definitely given her PTSD. I'm not sure how she overcame her fears at 54 years of age and moved to another country, but like her Uncle Jack, Mum just seemed to push through.

In 1948, she saved a young boy from drowning in a Nottingham Canal, near Clayton Bridge. When asked if she was scared, she replied, "I didn't have to do much."

Right before we left for Canada, I remember a partially deaf man and his family coming to the house. Later, I learned it was that boy she saved, and he had come to thank her.

On March 3, 1975, we boarded a British Airway 747

destined for Toronto's Pearson International Airport. The plane was so big inside, it felt like we were inside a huge flying house. This was the first time I'd been on a plane, so I was nervous, yet having Dad and Mum next to me made me feel safer.

It's funny because I still remember the in-flight movie, "*That's Entertainment.*" I vividly remember watching the film and trying to comprehend it, but it was made for adults.

Looking back, the film makes a lot of sense to me now. The movie feels like a message from my past. *That's Entertainment* was a celebration of the end of an amazing era. We all have eras in life that start and end, and this flight to Canada was the end of my childhood era in England. What I didn't know at the time, was that when you upend the apple cart, it takes a long time to get the apples back in place.

6
Oh, Canada

As the plane landed in Toronto, I could see the snow on the ground with huge piles stacked on the side of the runway.

Hmmm, snow ... That looks like fun! I thought to myself.

As we exited the plane onto the jet bridge, I felt the coldest cold ever, and I asked, "Dad it's freezing, is this normal?"

"Yes lad, Canada is extremely cold in the winter," he replied, smiling.

"What about the summer?" I asked, still shivering.

"It can be hot and humid," he responded.

Well, thank goodness it's March, I said. I'm sure it will warm up soon.

As we exited the gate, I was excited to see my sister. We had to go through international and immigration processing, which only made my anticipation greater. When we finally got to the main area of the airport, I could see Jennifer in the distance, and I ran as fast as I could to reach her.

"It's so good to see you!" she exclaimed, and she hugged all of us.

Finally, we're all back together, I thought to myself, but things would never be the same.

Our first month in Canada was spent with Jennifer and her husband, but their place was way too small for all of us. So they helped my Dad rent an apartment in Etobicoke on Brown's Line.

I remember staring out the apartment windows and being mesmerized by all of the traffic, the constant drone of cars and trucks, and the spaghetti shaped on and off ramps, that tied the huge highways together.

The move to Canada was tolerable at the start, but a big issue began rearing its ugly head as the weeks passed — my Dad's employment. Mum and Dad were starting to argue, and in our small Brown's Line apartment and there was no place to escape it. I couldn't just grab my football and go outside. There was no grass, just concrete and asphalt. It wasn't even safe.

Not even two months had passed, when my parents decided Toronto was too much of a culture shock for all of us. My older sister Glenise had been in Canada for about 10 years and had discovered an easier place to succeed in this new country.

They lived in a small farming town called Blenheim, Ontario, which is best known for hockey, farming, and not much else.

"Blenheim, what a nice little town, sounds like Bethlehem," said Mum, as we drove down Highway 401 to meet my sister and her family. As I gazed out the car window looking at the endless open fields of land, I couldn't believe the size, and how straight the roads were.

After about four hours of driving, we pulled into Blenheim. Glenise's house was built next to a church and directly across from the local curling club. I had no idea what curling was. At first, I thought it was a hairdresser.

Glenise and her husband Dennis had three younger kids, Andrew, Mandy, and Paul. Her family was very loving and it was quickly decided that Blenheim would be a better place to live than in the big city.

However, there were some positive things about the short time in Toronto. I saw my first ice hockey game at Maple Leaf Gardens, thanks to my brother-in-law, and I had my first slice of pizza at the Sherway Gardens. Both were epic and life-changing experiences, which somewhat softened the blow of moving to Canada.

Now in Blenheim, we stayed at Glenise's house, and Dad started working with Dennis doing interior and exterior painting and decorating. In England, my Dad was considered a master decorator, but in Canada, he was just a painter. However, it didn't take long for his employer, who was paying him almost minimum wage, to start billing him out at maximum rates.

Dad didn't care, he'd already owned his own company, and

he didn't want the stress of doing that again. He also didn't care about money, as long as we had what we needed, he was content to keep working as an employee. As I said, he was the best!

We'd only been in Blenheim about a week when I was told it was time to get back to school. By now, I'd missed almost three months, and my reading problems weren't getting any better.

After a full evaluation by the local public school, they placed me into the equivalent grade for my age. I have to admit, life definitely felt more normal, except for the fact that no one was playing football at recess. There were football goals, and nets, but the Canadian kids just didn't have the same passion to play the game as back in England.

At age 10, recess was more about swings, monkey bars, tag, and skipping rope. The school playground field wasn't small, but the grass was nowhere close to being as manicured as the grounds at Jesse Boot.

I also noticed these strange diamond shape fields that looked interesting,

Must be baseball, I thought to myself. A summer sport, I had been told.

As the school year of 1975 came to an end, my new teacher, Mrs Smith, turned out to be an angel. Like Mrs Grant, she knew nothing about my undiagnosed medical issues, yet she was able to provide me with some skills to help with linear reading, which had been impossible in years past.

My brain would jump around the page from line to line pulling out and connecting content. However, when the teacher asked me to stand up and read out loud, I couldn't.

As you can imagine, these types of disorders can crush one's confidence and we all know, kids can be mean. Sadly, this amazing teacher was killed shortly after in a car accident, giving me my first experience with the death of someone I really cared for.

After about six months had passed, my parents bought their own house, and I now had to navigate the streets to school. It wasn't very far to walk, but my route was fraught with several bullies that lived along the way.

Fortunately, I used to walk to school with my friend Mark, who lived across the main highway. Mark, was far more mature than his age, probably because he had three older brothers. He was the only one of my "so-called" friends that didn't tease my accent and call me a limey. However, like Gloss in England, he was a character in his own right. He was a prankster, an athlete, a musician, and sharp as a whip. Eventually, he became a very successful medical doctor but could've easily been a stand-up comedian.

Prank phone calls were rampant in the 1970s and '80s, and I'm sorry for anyone that missed that era. It was quite entertaining, to say the least.

Mark could easily change his voice, from a kid to a man, to a woman. We would spend hours combing the phone book and messing with our friends.

"Hello. Is John in the house?"

"No."

"Well, where do you go then? In the sink?" ☺

Every day, our trip home from school had some sort of adventure, and depending on which route we took, the action could be more than we bargained for.

It was during this time, I learned that not all Canadians are as warm and friendly as the welcoming reputation that precedes them.

One of our paths home ran right by the house of a huge kid — we'll call him Shrek, and keep his name anonymous. Shrek was a couple of years older, and he didn't like us. Every afternoon was like trying to get past a mean, nasty ogre.

Shrek would block the street, Mark would go one way, and I'd go the other. Then he'd try to chase one of us down, screaming. Usually, it was me, but luckily I was pretty fast.

Shrek would growl, "I'll get you tomorrow, especially you, you little limey bastard!"

He never, seemed to go after Mark with the same vigour,

probably because Mark was bigger than me, and he also had three brothers. I was always thankful Mark was there, or I would've taken a butt-kicking almost every day.

One night, I decided to play tennis after school with my friends. Mark didn't play tennis, so I had made plans to meet him back at his house for dinner with his family.

The late afternoon was beautiful, the air was warm and it was almost dusk. My hands were still wet from the sweat of playing tennis, which made it difficult to hold the racquet and ride my bike with one hand.

So, as we all did back then, I started riding with no hands. As I came around the corner onto Sheldrick Street, I wasn't really thinking about anything. I certainly wasn't thinking about Shrek, because it was much later and he was never on Sheldrick Street.

However, right at that instant, he stepped out from behind a parked car, directly in front of me, and stopped my bike cold in its tracks.

"Well, well, well. Where's your buddy?" he asked, and he shook the handlebars of my bike, back and forth.

"He's at home, that's where I'm going," I replied.

"You aren't going anywhere," he chuckled, obviously enjoying every moment.

"Come on, let me go," I pleaded.

Then he looked down and snatched the tennis racquet out

of my sweaty hand, "What's this piece of crap?"

"You know what it is, give it back," I begged.

Then he threw the racquet into the backyard two houses over. Shrek had just made a huge mistake. That racquet was one of the first gifts my Mum and Dad had bought me since leaving England and I was no longer afraid. I was angry.

"MY MUM BOUGHT THAT FOR ME," I shouted.

"Your Mummy, what are you going to do, you little baby," he taunted, then he tried to strike me in the face. I couldn't believe how long it took for the punch to arrive. It was like being in a slow-motion movie, as my Granddad's voice echoed in my head, "Lift your bloody hands, Stephen!"

His fist hit my raised hands — SMACK!

Shrek was now very angry that he missed his mark, which happened to be my face. Furious, he dragged me off my bike and I tripped over the frame onto the ground.

As I lay on the side of the road, I noticed a bit of sand beside me and grabbed a handful before standing up.

"YOU WANT MORE!" he screamed, as he came at me again.

"YOU'RE DONE!" I yelled, and I tossed the sand in his face and turned on the offensive.

I don't clearly remember the remaining details of the fight, only that he wasn't standing when it was over, and I was completely covered in blood — Shrek's blood.

In retrospect, my Granddad knew this day would come, and

he knew it would change my life forever. That's why his punch in the nose was the last valuable gift of love he could give me before I left for Canada.

That was also the last time Shrek would bully any of us. Our bully was defeated, I had learned how to scrap, and my English accent was slowly fading away.

However, just when you think things are settling down into a comfortable groove, that's when life can turn on you. For the first time, I felt what it was like to have power over another — and it felt better than being pushed around. It was the dark side, rearing its ugly head to greet me. Just like in *Star Wars*, once Anakin experiences revenge, he likes the power and the dark side enters him. Without that, we don't have Darth Vader. This can happen to any of us, as we conquer our bullies or get revenge on others for their wrongdoings. That negative energy somehow gets transmitted from them to you, maybe because of the direct, primal confrontation.

I later learned that Shrek's Dad was very abusive, so it made sense why that evil energy kept coming out through him. Many years later, I saw Shrek at the pub. He was sitting on a stool, with his huge body leaning over the bar. What's sad is he looked totally defeated. That's one of those times when you realize love is the only answer.

That night, I went over to him and we had a beer together. In Canada, beer is a sign of real love, Eh!

7

One in a Million

*T**he play between** light and darkness in this life never seems to end and as I aged into my early 20s, I became quite bitter with life, mostly due to my own doing. The last thing I wanted was another failure. I'd already had a failed first marriage and a failed first business, all within a short four-year period after high school.

My new plan was to keep things simple. Plus, due to my financial instability, I probably didn't come across as much of a catch.

It was during this period, I started to only care about weightlifting. I've never been a large guy, yet funny enough, I still bounced bars for years to help me get through school. I never tried to start scraps, but I definitely never shied away from one. Especially when my friends or bar patrons were at risk. I also never condoned fighting, it should be the last option for defence, but I'll admit it, a chip had formed on my shoulders, and the dark side energy was eating me from the inside out.

It was the Halloween weekend of 1987, and my good friend Fitzy had called me up and asked me to come into town from school. I wasn't bouncing that weekend, and I had nothing planned. So I jumped into my beat-up Toyota Corolla, with only one windshield wiper, and made my way out to rural southwestern Ontario.

As we walked into our favourite hangout, my eyes crossed paths with the girl I'd never seen before. It was so different, her eyes seem to penetrate my heart. We both looked back at each other, as she left the bar.

The next night was Halloween, and Fitzy and I decided to start the night off at another drinking establishment, but I couldn't stop thinking about those eyes.

"I wonder if she's at the other place?" I asked.

"Who?" replied Fitzy sarcastically, but he knew exactly who I was talking about.

"You know the one I saw last night," I replied, and we both leaned against the bar, showing off our cheesy Halloween costumes. Fitzy was dressed as Crockett (Don Johnson) from the Miami Vice TV show and I was dressed as Rambo. Nope, we weren't very creative that night. I could hear my Granddad say, "What a couple of berks!"

Anyhow, Fitzy was a great pal, and he could tell I was entranced with that unknown girl, and he knew where I wanted to go.

"OK, my friend, let's go see if we can find her," and finished his drink.

"Do you think she'll be there?" I asked.

"Well, we won't know unless we go there, will we," he laughed, still trying to act like Don Johnson.

"Alright Crockett," I chuckled, and we took off down the road to the last place I'd seen her.

As we entered the other bar, I immediately noticed the same girl sitting in the exact same chair, where coincidently I had the beer with Shrek sometime before.

She was sitting with another woman, Marg, who Fitzy just happened to know, and we were quickly introduced.

"Hi, my name is Laurie."

Still in shock that she was actually in my presence, I replied, "Hi, I'm Steve."

Laurie was dressed up as a country girl and she was simply stunning. The only thing that was going through my head was, don't say something stupid and screw this up. What I didn't know at the time, was she had also come back to see if I would return.

Somehow, we got on the topic of school, and we talked for hours about psychology, sociology, and even the study of rocks. That should be in the "Guide to Finding a Wife."

Seriously though, it was like I'd known her all my life. The conversation was effortless and meaningful — definitely no pickup lines and primal posturing.

As we kept chatting her presence seemed to wash away some of the dark energy in my heart. I could literally feel the anger inside me dissipate, like cool water on a raging fire.

In hindsight, the negative energy that surrounded me had been accumulating way before Shrek and far after. It was the build-up of every conflict I'd ever been in and there were a lot.

As fate would have it, I discovered Laurie was a behavioural counsellor at one of the high schools. How appropriate that the woman I would spend the rest of my life with, was professionally trained to deal with the likes of me.

Looking back, it was moments like these that make me realize how interconnected everything is, especially when seen through the lens of love and compassion.

Three years later, Laurie and I were married, with two girls to arrive over the next five years. Life's trajectory during this period was like a rocket. Probably not like the meteoric career of Great Uncle Jack during his glory days of wartime battles and championship runs, but for me, it was still very intense.

During that time, I received a strange call from my old friend, Mark, from Blenheim. He had moved to Toronto with his family when we were in high school.

"How are you, brother," he asked.

Mark made a great doctor because he always seemed to care about your well-being.

"I'm doing fine," I replied.

"What about Laurie and the family," he asked.

"They're good too," I continued.

"Well, I've moved back into your neck of the woods and I'm working ER at the local hospital, I'd love to see you," he explained.

"I'd love to see you too, when?" I asked.

Soon after, we started hanging out again. We quickly learned that we had both started amateur bodying building in our late teens. Another coincidence. Now closer to 30, we were both looking for something different.

One Saturday night, Mark, his girlfriend, Laurie and I, went to a party at my friend Marty's place. As we stood around his kitchen, Marty mentioned a new club he had recently joined in the city.

"Hey, you guys, I just joined a Jujitsu club!"

"Jujitsu, really, that sounds cool," I declared.

"Where's it located?" asked Mark.

"It's on Tecumseh Road, close to Pillette," he replied.

I'd taken several other styles of martial arts in the past, but had never found them to be that effective in real situations. However, I'd heard great things about Jujitsu and Judo and this sparked both of our interests.

"What does it entail?" I asked.

"Well it's Jujitsu, but some Judo. Basically, a lot of grappling, holds, and throws. They even teach you how to fall without getting injured," Marty explained, enthusiastically.

Mark and I looked at each other and finished our drink. We really didn't need to hear anymore. We were sold, and the next week we became members of the club. The sensei's name was Tom and the club produced some serious talent including, his son who was in the Olympics for Judo, and another fighter who was in the early UFC. The club had students from many different disciplines, including Muay Thai, Taekwondo, Isshinryu, Judo, etc. People came from all over Windsor to fight against other martial art styles. The competition was controlled but fierce, and Mark and I loved it.

Being one of the first true mixed-martial-arts clubs during that time, it still wasn't about being tough and fighting. It was about pushing through while still, maintaining honour, discipline, love and respect for others.

One night, sensei brought in an outside fighter. He was very soft spoken wearing a black belt and a black karate gi. As our session started, sensei looked at the class and said,

"Who would like to grapple against our new student?"

As I looked him over, he seemed overweight, and definitely in his 40s.

"Well," sensei asked again.

"Sure, I'm up for that," I replied, quite confidently, and I walked onto the mat, in front of my ageing opponent.

The grapple started slow.

I don't want to go too aggressive with the old guy, I thought to myself, as we both slowly moved in and out. As I gained confidence, I moved in and securely grabbed his gi and tried a foot sweep.

Suddenly, in less than a second I was flying through the air like a ragdoll and landed about eight feet away from him.

What the heck just happened, I thought as I lay flat on the thin mat.

I'd grappled against many fighters and I'd never experienced anything like that in my life. As laid there on my back, I could now hear everyone chuckling, including the sensei and of course, Mark.

Then I realized something was up.

"OK, who are you?" I asked, trying to get up.

The man smiled pulling me to my feet and placing his arm around me. It turned out he wasn't just into karate, he was a champion in Judo, and a Detroit cop to boot.

Granddad and Uncle Jack were definitely watching and chuckling along that day. But like the punch in the nose, I needed Shrek's chip knocking off my shoulder, and I believe they used sensei to do it.

I learned a lot from that club and those experiences, but what I remember the most wasn't my wins. It was my quick loss to the cop from Detroit that provided the mettle I needed, to not judge a book by its cover.

Shortly after we left Canada and moved to Michigan and just like that, my family were immigrants once again.

8

The Beautiful Game

*F*ive days before** the 1912 FA Cup Finals, the Titanic
sank. When the dreadful news reached England, there was little
room to be thinking about football, as people on both sides of
the Atlantic began counting their dead.

But as the days passed, stalwart fans along with most of the
general public were more than ready for a little distraction to
take them away from the unthinkable disaster of that
unsinkable ship.

Unfortunately, Barnsley fans would have to wait a little
longer before popping the cork on any victory celebration. For
West Bromwich Albion and Barnsley battled to a 0-0 tie in front
of over 54,000 fans at Crystal Palace in a defensive-driven final
match held on April 20.

It wouldn't be until the rematch four days later that
Barnsley would get a second crack at the title. But, if their
supporters were looking for a high-energy, high-scoring game,
they were sorely disappointed.

It was a hot, sunny April day and Albion did its best to

elevate the gameplay from a purely defensive struggle, but the scoring chances were few and far between. And when the chances did come, Albion couldn't take advantage of them. Pailor and Shearman missed a centring pass provided by Jephcott. Later in the second half, Pailor almost got a shot past Cooper, who failed to control the ball. It was defender Glendenning who saved the day for Barnsley by clearing the ball past the touchline, ending Albion's attempt at a goal.

On the Barnsley side, right winger Bartrop tested the Albion goalkeeper, Baddeley, who fumbled a save and nearly scored before the ball was kicked away by Albion fullback Pearson.

Other than his one, fumble-fingered play, Jack Cooper stood his ground and prevented Albion from scoring at all. It was his focused, consistent presence on the pitch that helped keep the score 0-0 as the game ran into extra time.

It was impressive that despite the hot, sunny conditions, both teams maintained such a heightened level of intensity for ninety minutes. It was clear that Albion was pushing the envelope the entire match, pressuring Cooper at every turn, bending him every which way without ever breaking the spirit of the tenacious goaltender. Minus a brief Barnsley attack by Travers and Moore, the offensive play was all Albion until the last two minutes of extra time.

In those added minutes, Barnsley's luck would change and the fate of the scrappy club would be one for the history books.

In those final moments, Glendenning dribbled the ball out of a crowd on the Barnsley side of the pitch, passing the ball to Tufnell who was already at midfield. Three Albion players surrounded the fleet striker as he cut through their constricting defensive formation.

Pennington, Cook, and Buck all failed to stop Tufnell as he approached the Albion goal. Keeper Pearson came out of the goal mouth trying to cut off the angle, stomping his feet like a madman in an attempt to knock the attacking forward off his game.

But, in the end, it was no use. Tufnell rocketed a perfect strike — fast, low, and right in the corner of Albion's net.

The Barnsley players rushed Tufnell, nearly knocking him off his feet with their hearty head rubs and joyful embraces. For the team knew they could hold off the Albion forces for another few minutes, and did so successfully. As the final whistle blew, Barnsley could finally lift the cup high, knowing they could finally be crowned — FA Cup Champions.

The trip back toward Sheffield was made by a parade of motor cars. But before the team left the Bramhall Lane pitch, they showed a bit of true class, taking a collection from the 38,555 fans for the Titanic Disaster Fund.

The procession through Sheffield was one for the ages.

Supporters and towns folk alike cheered for the conquering heroes as they lifted the cup high for all to see.

The reception in Barnsley was even greater, as staunch backers showed up in force to congratulate the returning victors, filling the main street with cheers and shouts of unbridled joy.

Jack Cooper happily joined his mates as the entire team presented the match ball to Tiverton Preedy, the reverend who had founded the club in the late 1800s. Preedy was so proud of his boys that he displayed the precious ball in his home until his death in 1928.

That day would shine in the memory of old Jack. Many would be the evening you could find him in the pub, recalling the glorious moment he helped lead his team to the ultimate victory. No one ever tired of hearing him tell of the tale of that storied season — the year Jack Cooper and the Tykes won it all.

9

Football or Soccer

Moving is hard and I never want to do it again, especially moving everything to another country.

It was the late 1990s, and after two years of searching for a house in a seller's market, Laurie and I finally agreed to build a house on an empty lot we found in north Oakland county.

It was around lunch when I got the call from my sister.

"Stephen, it's Jennifer."

"Hi Jennifer, how are you?" I replied. We hadn't spoken for quite a while, so I was concerned about the call.

"I'm fine, but I've got something to tell you. Unfortunately, it's not good news," she explained.

"What, what is it?"

"It's Andrew, he committed suicide in Toronto."

"What!"

I stood in our bedroom and I broke down, still holding onto the phone. I hadn't cried like that since I was a child. Andrew was my sister, Glenise's oldest, who we lived with when we first came to Canada. Her kids were more like my brothers and sister than my nephews and niece. Andrew "Milsy" was a great guy, and everyone loved him. I actually saw Milsy, at a bar, shortly before this tragedy. I remember trying to speak with him, but as I looked into his eyes, he was already gone. The anger and stress of this world had totally consumed him.

After I ended the call with Jennifer I tried to compose myself, and I dialled the president of the company who'd employed me for the last 10 years and moved us from Canada.

"Hi Mike, it's Steve."

"Yes, Hi Steve, are you OK?" he could obviously tell from my voice that something was wrong.

"No, I'm not, my nephew just passed away, unexpectedly, I'm going to need some time off," I explained.

"I'm so sorry, Steve, take all time you need," he replied.

Mike was a family man, a good man, and he'd been great to my family and I. The problem was, I was tired. I was tired of fighting his internal company battles, in a dog-eat-dog corporate culture. Most importantly, I was tired of the negative energy that I believed was stealing my life and was hurting my relationship with Laurie and my family.

Two weeks later, I resigned and we started our own business. I'm frankly not sure why I thought owning a business would decrease my stress level. I'd owned a business before and it failed, so why would this be any different?

Well, it wasn't and by not selecting the right business

partners and making rookie start-up business decisions, we barely made it. For several years we continued to struggle, until Laurie and I figured out how to make it work.

However, there is one major benefit to owning your own business, and that is the flexibility of time, and time is definitely what our children needed.

My girls were born in Canada and we moved when Noelle was 2 years old and Lindsey was 6 months old. They were incredible kids, very loving, kind, and well-rounded. As the girls reached certain ages, it was their life events that allowed me to start seeing the connections between different moments in time and space. It was almost like Uncle Jack, my Dad, Granddad and Andrew, were all saying,

"It's time to wake up and focus on your family, lad!"

♦

It was 2005, Lindsey was nine and Noelle was 11. Both my daughters were playing softball and I was helping as the assistant coach. The head coach, by the way, looked and acted a lot like Shrek. During one of our games, I had to stop him and the other team's coach from getting into a fistfight over a chirping noise an 8-year-old player was making.

"What on earth is the matter with you guys, these are just

little kids," I yelled, as I pushed them apart.

I thought to myself, *If this is the behaviour in rec, then I can't imagine what travel softball must be like.*

At the end of the season, Laurie and I agreed, to no more softball, and I was relieved.

The following winter was nice and calm and as we moved into the spring I was enjoying my free time.

This is when I got the call from above.

"Hey, what are you doing?" Laurie asked.

"I'm driving to the office, what's up?" I replied.

"Oh, nothing. I just thought I'd let you know, I signed up the girls for soccer," she explained.

"Soccer? You mean football," I replied.

"OK, football," she laughed.

"Well, at least it's not softball."

"Yeah, that's for sure, but there's a problem,"

"What problem?" I asked.

"Well, they don't have a coach for the Under-10 team!"

I thought to myself, *Hmmm, I see where this is going.*

"Sorry, but there's no way I'm coaching, softball was enough, I'm retired," I insisted.

"Well, if you don't, then Lindsey can't play, beside you grew up in England and you probably know this game better than most of the other parents in the league."

I wasn't thrilled about the thought of coaching anything

after last season, but there was something intriguing about football, and I really did miss the game, especially if played correctly, outside, and on grass.

I sighed and asked, "Where are the games and practices at?"

"Outside at the Civic Centre and Friendship Park," she explained.

"Hmmm, at least close to home and the office," I replied.

"So, can I put your name down?" she asked.

"Yep, do it," I agreed.

"OK thanks, bye," and she ended the call.

I've never coached football before, I thought to myself. *But it's nothing too crazy, it's just rec.*

The season started fast. At first, I was just coaching Lindsey because of their age difference and Noelle was on another team. During the first season, I had a decent group of players, and we won quite a few games. To my surprise, I was having a lot of fun and loved the action, especially compared to watching the last two years of Under-10 softball.

Noelle and Lindsey were fairly decent at softball, but they definitely seemed to have more of a knack for football, and as they got older, their skills and the level of competition increased significantly.

Unfortunately, I had to start calling it soccer, for communication purposes, even though it bothered the heck out of me, but what could I do? When in Rome!

10

Called Back Home

*T**he entire football*** coaching experience, got my mind thinking, and I started to dream about Nottingham. Late one night, I couldn't get it out of my mind, so I went downstairs to the computer and started to search for Nottingham-related topics. As I surfed over a few websites, I noticed a link for a men's Nottingham ice hockey league.

Ice hockey, in England, I thought to myself, as I clicked on the link. At first, the teams in the league popped up and for some reason, I started clicking on the rosters of each team. As I read the names, I was stunned to find, *Gloss's full name,* at the top of the list.

"There's no way, that's my old mate," I mumbled to myself, and clicked on his name.

"HOLY CRAP!" I said out loud. There was his picture, older, but it was definitely Gloss. I fell back in my chair, blown away.

As I navigated down the page, I saw a team manager email button. So I wrote him a note, asking him if Gloss went to Jesse Boot Primary School, and if he knew me.

SEND.

I even woke Laurie up to tell her. She probably thought I was nuts.

The next day, I received a reply, and it read, "Yes, I believe he did go to Jesse Boot and I'll be seeing him tonight at training. I'll let you know if he remembers you."

"Thanks," I responded, and I waited.

The following day, I received another email.

"Mate, he knows who you are and wants to talk to you as soon as possible. Here is his number."

I couldn't believe it. What are the chances? I hadn't spoken to him since I left his grandmother's house on that day 30 years ago and now he's playing ice hockey in England.

Are you serious, I thought to myself.

So, the next day, I called him, and we talked for hours. It was like no time had passed. He had played semi-professional football and blew out his knee, and his boys had started playing ice hockey, which got him into coaching at the Nottingham Ice Centre.

Meanwhile, I, on the other hand, was playing ice hockey in the USA and coaching football. What a flip-flop. I wouldn't even want to calculate the odds of this. It would be ridiculous. So, my family decided to plan a trip to England in the summer of 2006.

The first time back in 30 years.

The only reasonable flights were out of Canada, so we had to drive from Michigan to Toronto, and then fly into Birmingham. Upon arrival in the UK, Gloss picked us up at the airport and everything from that point forward was surreal.

As we followed the roundabout and headed into the countryside, I was filled with so many emotions and didn't know how to process them. Feelings of joy, closure, love and a reality check all combined into one package. I could hear a voice saying, "See, you weren't dreaming. Your past is real."

Who's talking to me? I thought to myself.

The following nine days were like a fairy tale and on top of that, it was also the World Cup, and English flags were hanging from almost every house.

Gloss had taken the entire week off and drove us all around. It seemed like everywhere we visited, in Nottingham, both our last names were somewhere on the display.

I'm definitely home, I thought to myself.

As you get older, it's interesting what defines a perfect day. On the last Sunday of our trip, both our families decided to visit one of my favourite places in Nottinghamshire, Sherwood Forest and the Major Oak tree. After we walked through the forest we came to a manicured playing field called the Edwinstowe Cricket Grounds. For the next few hours, our families, kicked the football around and played a bit of cricket. It was a perfect day and it brought me right back to how we used to play as kids.

The next day we visited Belvoir Castle and we brought my Aunt Edna with us. Edna was my Mum's only surviving sister and quite a character. She had a great sense of humour and was sharp as a tack for any age, especially almost ninety. As we toured the castle I thought, *wow, two perfect days in a row. Magical.*

As the trip wound down, I didn't want to leave England again. It was such an enchanted experience, especially being able to share it with my wife and daughters.

As we entered the airport departure gate, I looked back at Gloss and his family, and I had the same sad feeling that I had when I left in 1975.

Laurie could easily read my body language and she grabbed my hand and said, "It's OK, we will come back again."

During the next year Laurie had a hip replacement, so I doubted we would get back to England anytime soon. My biggest concern was her health, but she certainly showed her mettle, and only eight weeks after her surgery, we went to England for two weeks, where she walked miles on her new hip.

This time our family really fell in love with Gloss's family and my Aunt Edna.

During a visit to Edna's flat, we were drinking tea and talking, when I mentioned that I was coaching Lindsey in football, and Noelle was playing goal.

As Edna listened, she then said, "Well you know, I got it, right?"

"Got what?" I replied. Confused.

"Well, you know, I'll show ya," and she left the room. After a couple of minutes had passed, she came back in with what looked like a jewellery case. Now we were all confused.

"It's Jack's medal, Stephen, I have it," she claimed.

"You whut?" I responded, still remembering it around my Grandma's neck.

"Here, open it," and she handed it to me.

"OK," I replied nervously as I lifted the hinged lid.

Inside, lay three medals, one, Alec Denman's retirement medal, two, Jack's runner-up FA cup medal from 1910, and three, the largest medal, Jack's 1912 FA Cup Championship medal. All the medals were in pristine condition. My family had kept them all this time, through two World Wars, the Great Depression, and various other calamities.

The bottom line was that these medals were priceless to our family's history. As we were leaving, she whispered to me, "You know, I'm not going to be around for much longer, and I need someone I can trust to take these medals. I trust you Stephen, and you coach football, you would take care of them."

At first, I was speechless because I knew the responsibility I was being given.

"Of course, I would, but you're not going anywhere yet, Aunty, " I smiled, and we gave her a hug and we left her flat.

About a year past before she called me again. She sounded frantic, and very concerned about the security of the medals. So, I got a flight from Detroit and set off for Nottingham.

Upon arrival, Gloss picked me up and took me directly to see her. As we entered her flat, I could tell her health was failing, and I knew this might be the last time I would see her. She made me a nice cup of tea, with lots of milk and handed me the package containing all the medals, and she hugged me.

"They will be safe with me, Aunty."

"Thank you, Stephen, thank you so much," she replied, and we continued to chat for hours.

As I sat on the plane on the way back to the USA, I couldn't stop thinking about Jack, and what the game must have been like in 1912. It had been stated many years ago by Jack's daughter, that if the medals couldn't stay with family then they should go back to the team, if possible.

So I thought, *what if we could go back to Barnsley and talk to the team administration?*

11

Through The Mud

*O*nce we got home from England, my stress levels and anxiety seemed to be increasing. I'd always had some sort of low-level feeling of anxiety. You know that feeling in your stomach, that tries to stop you from doing things? However, something was different this time and the feeling was more intense.

A couple of months later, I was asked by my former Marine buddy, to run a 12-mile obstacle race in Ohio, called Tough Mudder. Forgetting my age, I accepted the challenge and signed up on the website.

The day of the event was in April, and the weather was rainy and in the low 40s. Besides the cold, I just didn't feel my normal self and had just gotten over the flu the week prior.

The first six miles were without incident, but at mile six, I jumped up onto the monkey bar obstacle and started to move forward. My hands kept slipping on the wet muddy rungs, so I grabbed the outside rails of the wooden structure.

This is a lot easier, I thought to myself, but right at that moment, I heard the wood starting to break, — SNAP.

Wow, the beams are breaking, I thought to myself as looked down at the dirty water below. Then a second SNAP, and I realized that it wasn't the wood making that sound, it was my arm, and I dropped into the water.

As I swam to the other side, I knew that I had completely ripped off my bicep, and I climbed out to assess the damage. The muscle tendon was in a little ball and luckily my arm felt numb from the cold water. I remember my friend, Chuck, saying, "There's a mobile ambulance over there, go see them."

It was at that split second, I watched a man with an artificial leg run past us, and I replied, "No, I want to finish!"

"Are you sure?" asked Chuck, obviously concerned.

"Yes, I'm sure," I replied. "Let's go," and we continued on to finish the final six miles.

I learned a lot that day, especially during the last two hours. God does carry you when you can't go on, and he'd been doing it all my life. Granddad, Dad, Uncle Jack, and Andrew were definitely cheering me on across the finish line.

The next day I arrived home, but nobody was around. So I grabbed a lawn chair and waited on the driveway for my family to return.

A little while later, they pulled in and immediately jumped out of the vehicle to see me. They knew I'd been injured and I hugged them, and it was probably the first time they'd ever seen me emotional. It was tears of appreciation to be home and have them in my life.

At the time, I thought I was fairly healthy, so I chalked it up to a fluke accident, and had surgery to have the bicep muscle reattached. Later the next year, my right knee went out and I had to have another surgery. Again, I disregarded it.

Just wear and tear, I thought to myself.

A year later, I ripped my tricep off playing ice hockey from a very simple fall. This injury stopped me from doing everything, including full-time work.

As I tried to rehab my arm after the tricep surgery, my eyes started to lose focus at far distances combined with strange hallucinations. I still just thought it was all a part of ageing.

Six months later, I started to have more hallucinations and out-of-body type experiences that put me in the hospital for four days. After a battery of tests for petite mal seizures, everything came back normal and they sent me home. So, I went back at the optometrist still complaining about my eyes, and wondering if they were causing my hallucinations.

"Do you have problems reading?" asked my optometrist, Dr Debbie.

I laughed, "Yes, I have a form of dyslexia, I think."

"Dyslexia, who told you that?" she asked.

"Several people over the years, I don't know, some days are worse than others," I replied.

"Try reading now with these lenses," she said and placed a pair of glasses on my head. Instantly, it was like someone had removed a filter from my brain and I could read almost perfectly.

Dr Debbie explained my eyes were vertically misaligned and that's why my brain was looking at different lines of text at the same time and mixing up the words. Over the next few appointments, she also noticed that my eyes had different readings every time she examined me, so she started to ask deeper questions.

"Have you ever had a concussion?"

"Well I've played a lot of sports, had a couple of motorcycle accidents, and definitely taken a few punches over the years," I replied, laughing.

"I'm going to send you to a neurologist, I think there's more going on than just your eyes," she explained.

By the time I got in to see the neurologist, my symptoms were becoming very serious. After a quick diagnosis, the neurologist sent me over to a Detroit-based endocrinologist, who handles concussions for professional football and hockey players. After a four-hour blood test, the endocrinologist diagnosed me with hypopituitarism (aka secondary Addison's disease), which apparently President John F. Kennedy also had. After the test, the doctor quickly entered the room and sat beside me.

"Listen carefully, your cortisol and GH levels are non-existent, probably one of the worst cases I've seen in quite a while. If we don't get this turned around you probably won't live longer than four to six months."

As I listened to him, I sat there in disbelief. How could this be, I'm fairly young, I work out, and I eat healthy.

"Well, what can we do to change this,?" I asked.

"Medication, especially hydrocortisone," he replied. "Your body isn't producing any and that's why you're so stressed and feel anxious all the time."

Now it was all making sense!

"You've probably had Addison's all your life and you didn't know it, and as you get older, it sneaks up on you," he explained.

Losing the use of my arms was not fun, but losing my mind was very scary, to say the least, and this disorder side-lined me for a while.

The medication the endocrinologist prescribed changed my life in so many ways, that even my vision came back. I felt very blessed to have a real second chance at life.

I've always been a curious person and some of my hallucinations were unbelievably real. I would actually see full scenes containing people I didn't even know. As I tried to focus on the scene it would make me feel like I was about to throw up. So during my illness, I started to write about what I was experiencing, and the end result was very unusual.

Somehow, even while injured, my brain was able to connect beyond my own consciousness and create stories. I used many of my own, wild out-of-body experiences to write a fiction novel.

It's so strange because when I go back to read my book, it feels like I didn't even write it. Might sound crazy, but it's true. I truly believe we are all connected beings, linked through a higher consciousness to our loved ones in other dimensions.

And that is the beauty of this part of the story. For it was not through my strengths that I was developing true mettle. It was through all my weaknesses.

I would've never started writing if things had not happened the way they did, and without that, I would have never reconnected with the spirits of my ancestors, like Uncle Jack, my Dad, Granddad, and Andrew.

Later, we found out that one of my daughters also had Addison's, and fortunately she didn't have to go so many years undiagnosed.

Life is an amazing journey of discovery and sometimes that discovery is hiding right inside your own mind, waiting to be revealed.

12

Whatever Happened to Baby Jack?

*I**t seemed that** Jack Cooper (Holloway), born in Sneinton, Nottingham, came into this world in a pair of nubby football boots, and even after his glory years with Barnsley, Jack could never get the game out of his blood.

After that championship season, Cooper continued to play for his favourite club until the onset of the First World War, where he served in France with the Royal Field Artillery division.

Even in times of global conflict, Jack couldn't get the football bug out of his system. During the war, he played for Arsenal in a makeshift league until regular play resumed four years later.

On the resumption of league games, Cooper joined Newport County in the new Southern League in the third division. Jack was the keeper in the inaugural match against Reading in August of 1920, and played for another two seasons, making over 100 appearances before his retirement in 1922.

Whether on or off the pitch, Jack Cooper was known as a tenacious, strong-minded person, who was always ready to step in and help out where he could.

During the war, he was a machine gunner. His fellow soldiers relied on him to provide cover during battle and at times of attack. Jack would use his natural ability to "see the field" to direct fire in the proper direction while ensuring that his own men were given a sporting chance on the battlefield.

After the war, Cooper retired to Nottingham, where he was known to be a very thoughtful, generous person. Though he maintained his fierce competitiveness in darts and horse racing, Jack was always there to stick up for the less fortunate and downtrodden.

During that post-war period, supplies were low and many people were starving and struggling to make ends meet. At that time, the government passed a law that no one could hunt for their own food unless they already owned at least £100 worth of property. Jack knew this law to be discriminatory and unfair, so just like the fictional Robin Hood, he went ahead and poached enough game to feed numerous families in the town over the course of many months.

He was never arrested.

In his later years, Cooper frequented the local pubs and

race tracks, making friends wherever he went. People of the town knew of his fame and he was seen as a respected icon throughout the community. On any given night, you could find Cooper sitting on a stool or in a booth in a local pub, spinning colourful yarns and grand stories deep into the night.

Eventually, in 1952, at the still young age of 64, Jack Cooper took his final breath on this earth and shuffled off his mortal coil, bound to tend to more lofty goals beyond the pearly gates. Jack left behind a loving family, a grateful town, and a legacy of tough, hard-fought success that lingers to this day across the English countryside.

13

You Can Go Home Again

What an absolutely beautiful summer day for a stroll in South Yorkshire, I thought to myself, as I glanced over at Laurie and my two teenage daughters walking alongside me.

"Go straight up Belgrave. It's right at the top," I explained, reiterating what a local at the pub, had told me.

Belgrave was a fairly plain street, lined with red brick houses on both sides and not much shrubbery. In comparison to the large expanse of Michigan, it almost felt like we were walking up through a tunnel. As we reached the top of the hill, I could now see the red wall of the iconic Oakwell Football Stadium.

Wow, the home of the Barnsley Football Club, I thought to myself.

"I wonder, which way it is to the front office?" I questioned, as we crossed over Grove Street and approached the old structure.

"I'm not sure," replied Laurie.

Then Lindsey noticed an opening,

"Let's go this way," she suggested, and we followed her to the left. It quickly became apparent, that we were walking around the back of the building and not in the direction of the front office.

"Look the back gates are open," she noticed, pointing towards the rear of the stadium.

"I see that, but can we go in that way," I replied, but my daughters had already started to jog over to the gate.

"Let's go," said Laurie.

"There was no one in sight, are you sure we should be going this way," I replied, trying to keep us out of trouble.

"Come on Hun, what are they going to say," she smiled, and we proceeded through the gates, entering the huge empty stadium from what must have been the rear service entrance. Very quickly we found ourselves standing right next to one of the grandstands and only a yard from the actual pitch itself. Still cautious about being there without permission, I carefully walked towards the edge of the pristine pitch.

The sky was so blue it made all the colours seem even more vivid. The green, unmarked grass of the football pitch seemed to gleam in absolute perfection.

Kneeling down I felt the grass and thought to myself, *it's as if someone already knew we were coming, opened the gates, and guided us in.*

There we stood, directly on the edge of the same football

field, that my Great Uncle Jack Cooper had played, 100 years prior. I started to gaze at the old empty stands surrounding all four sides of the pitch and could feel the energy.

Great Uncle Jack was right there beside us. Our own guided tour was provided by the MVP and goalkeeper of the 1912 Barnsley Football Club. The only FA Cup championship in their franchise history.

I felt honoured to be there with my family, thousands of miles away from our home in Michigan. It was as if, time and space, past and present had connected, creating the perfect moment to truly appreciate Jack's Mettle.

It felt like a dream, and as I continued to scan the empty stands housed by the 125-year-old iconic structure, I tried to imagine the sound of singing and the roar of the crowd echoing in the silence.

"That's certainly strange, that the rear gates were open," I remarked.

"Yes, it looks like they're doing maintenance," Laurie replied, as they continued to wander the stands.

"Look, I see someone working over there," yelled Noelle.

"Good, let's ask him where the team office is," replied Laurie and we started walking towards the chap.

"Hello, we are looking for the team office, can you direct us," I asked.

"Sure Mate, just go back the way you came in, turn left, and walk around to the end of the stadium. It's right there," he replied in his distinct Yorkshire accent.

"Thank you," we replied and started to walk back through the large gates following his directions out the back and down the side of the stadium. As we came around the corner, we could see a front office and what seemed like a gift shop.

The store was the front of the head office and the marketing group.

"Hi, how are you? I asked the lady at the counter.

"I'm very well, how can I help you? she responded.

"Well that's a long story," I chuckled, and began to explain our relationship to Jack Cooper, the legendary Barnsley goalkeeper.

As I finished she smiled and said, "I've got something for you and she went through a door into the back.

Upon returning, she held a three-panel picture frame containing the entire 1912 Barnsley Championship team and a photograph of the game.

"We just made this in marketing for the 100th anniversary," she explained.

So there we were in 2012, 100 years from the anniversary of the game. I'm not a gambling man but what were the odds of that all that coming together, in one neat package — *Not bloody likely,* I thought.

When asked, the Barnsley front office stated that they had

no place to keep the medal and they suggested that the safest place to keep it was with the family.

That was the last time we were in Barnsley, but the memory of that day, on that pitch, with my family is burned into my memory like a warm fire, rekindled and comforting every time I recollect it.

Looking back, Noelle and Lindsey had both played keeper and that was before they knew anything about their famous relative. Both were great players, with solid boots, and like Great Uncle Jack, they had the warrior spirit. I carried both my girls off the pitch several times. Noelle even had her finger broken by a kick from a dirty striker and still finished and won the game. My daughters never complained, they just played and loved every minute.

I know Jack was always with them, and still is, and when my girls retired from playing at 16 years of age, I felt a huge loss. It was one of those era-ending type feelings like the message in that in-flight film, *That's Entertainment*.

Fortunately, life isn't a movie, and every day you're alive you can write another story. So one day, Noelle and I were talking about how I would miss coaching.

Then Noelle asked, "Why don't you coach another team?"

"But I don't have any kids on the team," I replied.

"So, why do need to have kids on the team?"

"I never really thought about it. I guess I don't. Why, do you want to help me coach?" I asked.

"Sure," she agreed, and that was that. I called the league the following week and they were happy to give us a team.

The next year, my Aunt Edna passed away and Laurie and I flew back to handle her estate. She was a class act and I miss her dearly.

RIP Aunty Edna!

14
At Last

*I*t's hard to **believe** a year has gone by, and there we were, standing on the same pitch in Michigan, staring down the same team once again.

It was a crazy season, full of ups and downs, injuries, family dramas, and even a few run-ins with the referee. But the players were wonderful and grew in skill and confidence greater than I could've ever imagined.

From the very beginning, I had told the team how important it was they play their own game and not worry about the opponent. If we played to the best ability, competed fairly, and had fun doing it, we may not win every game, but we would always be winners. These ideals served us well, and the team worked its way up to first place in the league. However, we needed to win one last game to solidify the championship.

The game began with its usual intensity, and it was clear that it was going to be a battle from start to finish.

Our goalkeeper, Shannon, was simply amazing. She stopped at least three breakaways in the first half and stymied their strikers at every turn.

On offence, our half-backs controlled the middle of the pitch, constantly feeding our forwards and setting up numerous scoring opportunities. Yet, despite so much forward progress, we were unable to put a ball in the back of the net deep into the second half.

The ebb and flow of the game went back and forth with neither team being able to score, but the other team was really starting to press. The referee signalled to both coaches that there were five minutes left in the final half. As the seconds ticked off in those final minutes, the girls on both sides pushed themselves to the limit, fiercely battling against fatigue and exhaustion.

Suddenly, Willow yelled from the pitch.

"Coach, my shoe just broke!"

"Are you serious?" I responded and quickly I subbed her out.

What a lousy time to lose our striker, I thought to myself.

As Willow sat down, Noelle calmly removed her own football boots and gave them to the young striker to lace up.

"They fit perfectly," smiled Willow.

Perplexed, I shook my head in disbelief and subbed her back in the game. Within seconds of returning to the pitch, our centre mid-fielder sent a toss that reached the right foot of Willow.

I felt something warm well up in my chest as I watched the striker move with speed and precision across the midline. There was only one defender to beat as she cut a clear path to the goal. Everyone on the sideline watched in wonder, as the entire scene moved in slow motion. She faked left and then sprinted past the last defender who struggled to tackle her from behind.

I braced myself, frozen, as the referee lifted the whistle to his lips, ready to sound the end of the game with three, long blasts.

In that fraction of a second, everything seemed to merge together. I tugged at the chain under my shirt, feeling the warm thing against my chest. All at once, my eyes blurred, unable to process the drama that played out before me. The last two things I heard were the roar from the sideline and the shrill, triple tweets from the referee's Fox 40 Classic. When I came to my senses, I was surrounded by a swarm of jumping, screaming players, shouting, "Yes! Yes! Yes! We did it!"

We had done it. We had won... One – Nil.

In the aftermath, everything came back into focus and Willow's final strike rested calmly in the back of the net.

It was an inconceivable experience, standing in front of players, trying to summarize the game and congratulate them on the entire season, while still trying to process our incredible victory.

As the impromptu ceremony ended, Willow noticed I had been fussing at the necklace hidden under my coach's jersey.

"Coach, what is it that you're wearing?" Willow questioned as I started walking towards the parking lot. She caught me off guard a little, as I paused, before lifting the object out from underneath my jersey, revealing Jack's medal to her for the first time.

My eyes welled up with tears, but I did my best to keep my composure as I answered, "That's a great question. I really didn't want anyone to know, but I wore this medal today as a sign of respect and remembrance for my family. This is my Great Uncle's Jacks championship medallion from 1912 when he was part of the Barnsley team that won the FA Cup in England."

Willow leaned over to take a closer look. "Wow, did it bring us luck?" she asked.

"Well, I have to admit, I definitely wanted Jack with us today. But, it means much more than luck. Just like the medals you won are a sign of the great things the team did this season.

As you grow older, these awards will become fond remembrances for you and your family. They are heirlooms that will hopefully spark a little pride and joy for your descendants in years to come."

Willow smiled holding her own medal around her neck.

"So be proud but be grateful and humble for what you have

achieved. For, I am grateful for you, and feel blessed to have had the honour to coach you this season, Willow."

"Thank you so much, Coach, I'll see you at indoor practice," she said and ran off towards her parents.

Then I remembered, I had forgotten to grab the corner flags. So I returned back to the empty pitch just as dusk was settling in. As I pulled out the first flag, I looked down the field along the freshly marked sideline. It reminded me of a road, and as I began to walk towards the second flag, I suddenly became ten years old again. I could clearly see Jesse Boot school and I could even sense the fog and wind on my face.

As I pulled out the second flag, the vision dissolved. However, now I could feel the energy of Jack, Dad, Mum, Edna, Andrew, Grandma and Granddad, creating a connection across time and space....*and I prayed, Dear God, I'm so appreciative to be where you placed me. Thank you, for allowing Great Uncle Jack to be there in my life, and to show me the real meaning of winning — the courage, perseverance, and fortitude to carry on despite all adversity.*

For the first time, I knew what it meant to be a part of a rich, family history. I finally understood what it meant to truly possess Jack's mettle.

The End

Epilogue

Goodbye sweet yesterday; Can you feel the winds of change? *Lyrics by British recording artist, Johnny Hates Jazz.*

As I sit here, quietly listening to music, I contemplate how to write this epilogue. How can these stories be brought together in a beautiful crescendo?

Well, as it turns out, the answer is simple. I don't need to; it has already been done for me.

Yesterday, we went to my daughter Noelle's house to pray over my new grandson Aidan. Since his birth, four months ago, Aidan has been experiencing physical complications. In addition to being born with Down syndrome, Aidan only has one heart valve. This type of disorder is common in people with Down syndrome and can be fixed with specialized surgery. Because he couldn't hold down any food, he was placed on a feeding tube and several medications for congestive heart failure.

The goal was for Aidan's parents, Noelle and Brian, to prepare him for tomorrow's open-heart surgery.

Mettle means a person's ability to cope well with difficulties or to face a demanding situation in a spirited and resilient way.

Aidan barely cries or fusses. He's truly a blessing and shows his mettle every day, and so do his parents.

After we got home, I started editing some of the first chapters of this story and something caught my attention. Jack Cooper was born, John Holloway, and then it hit me. Jack's real name is John and Aidan's middle name is Johnathan. Coincidence, I think not. Noelle and Brian didn't know that fact when they named Aidan.

I can't wait to hang Jack's medal around Aidan's neck after he recovers from his heart surgery.

... the winds have changed.

Cheers,

Stephen Sadler

Stories to be shared.